THE PROPOSITION

BRYAN FERRO

Vol. 3

H.M. Ward

www.SexyAwesomeBooks.com

H.M. Ward Press

COPYRIGHT

H.M. Ward Press
First Edition: March 2014
ISBN: 9781630350222

CHAPTER 1

Holy crap. It's like a sucker punch straight into the stomach. The air is forced out of my lungs and my jaw drops. Neil lifts the ring higher making the stone sparkle in the light. The ginormous diamond is larger than life and much more than he could possibly afford.

Cecily has her hands over her mouth in giddy excitement. She looks as if she wants to jump up and down. "Oh this is so exciting! Just think of the wedding!"

Neil is beaming at her before his gaze returns to meet mine. I haven't said anything yet and it's becoming noticeable. Our hands are touching, but it's uncomfortable. I don't like this. My stomach twists into knots. I don't know what I want. He's a good guy for the most part, but I've been through so much so fast that this scares me. I need time to think, but with Cecily there, I can't say that. What do I say? Finally, I stammer out, "Neil, I—"

Cecily mistakes my lack of words for something else and shoves Neil's shoulder. It's affirmation, a pat on the back. "See! You've rendered her speechless! Look at that! My little star ran out of words. Well, don't just stand there, Neil, put the ring on her finger." Cecily's scratchy voice comes with gusto and the huge-ass smile that lines her painted lips is going to crack her plastic face.

Neil does as he's told and I shiver as the cold band slides over my skin. It feels wrong, but I can't find the words. My mind picks the ring apart. Gently, it prods me: *The metal is the wrong color, the stone is the wrong shape, and this is the wrong guy.* The thought starts to form, but before it solidifies, Cecily blasts it to bits.

"Come along, I have them all waiting!" She grabs us both, pulling our wrists toward the back of the little house.

Neil tries to explain as he beams at me. "You're going to love it. Just wait, Hallie." Neil is wearing his Saturday date clothes— his favorite outfit with the button down white shirt, complete with French cuff links, and a bland tie. He's wearing a leather vest over it that's buttoned and pristine. Not a hair is out of place.

Leaning in, I try to whisper to Neil, but Cecily keeps talking over me, prattling about something she got for us. I'm thinking it's a present that she's pulling us toward, so I keep trying. "Neil, I need to talk to you. Neil?"

But he's all toothy smiles and laughing with Cecily as we're shoved out the back door. Then a barrage of flashing lights blinds me. Cecily's voice booms behind me into a microphone, "She said yes!"

CHAPTER 2

Holy shit! The yard is filled with people. They're everywhere. I'm blinded by lights and shield my eyes to see a sea of faces I don't recognize.

Neil tugs me to his side and holds up my hand. I barely have time to take in the reporters and Neil's friends before he grabs the microphone from Cecily. "This is the happiest day of my life. Here's to Hallie! I love you, baby."

Someone shoves a champagne flute in my hand and a band starts to play. The tiny yard is filled with little white lights, music, and food. It's a party. I blink again and realize what he's done. This is an engagement party. Neil clicks his glass to mine and takes a sip.

Holy rabid fuckbunnies. Why does he do stuff like this? I'm not ready for marriage. I would have waited, but now I don't have the choice. If I say something, I'll humiliate him and look like a bitch. I down the glass of champagne and laugh nervously. Tension lines my neck and shoulders as I plaster a fake smile on my face. I'll tell him later, I'll say no when everyone isn't around. I can fake it until then.

Cecily pulls me away and takes me to meet some industry people, but I've mentally left the party. My mind drifts back to Bryan. I wish things were different. I wish he was serious about me, but he's not. Neil's the one who wants to marry me. Maybe I should keep this ring, after all, if I give it back I'll be alone. Neil may not be perfect, but he's good enough, isn't he?

God, I wish Maggie were here. Where is she anyway? I stop the man who's been talking a mile a minute since Cecily walked me over. I waited and waited for him to come up for air and hush for a second so I could excuse myself.

I finally put my hand on his forearm and smile up at his wrinkled, round face. "Thank you so much, and I'd love to discuss this with you more at length, but I need to go see to something." Cecily looks mortified, but I walk away. More people take my picture as I shoulder my way through the crowd looking for Maggie. She has to be here. Neil wouldn't throw an engagement party without my best friend, but I don't see her.

Neil is standing with a group of his co-workers and as I approach, I can hear him saying, "It's all part of the psyche that lies dormant. Hallie is rational as they come. It was ingenious of her to consider the ramifications of leading such a feral lifestyle in her novel. I think that's why people are drawn to it, the book has that train wreck morbidity that renders people unable to look away—it's human nature."

He's smiling and all his friends are nodding along with him. What a bunch of pretentious, arrogant, tight-asses. Meanwhile, I'm sure there isn't one of them that wouldn't like to take a woman's ass or fuck her face. They're just too chicken to do it, or admit it. Neil makes me sound like a monster because my character enjoys such things, because I enjoy those acts of passion.

"Neil?" I sound like a little dormouse. My voice is barely a squeak. My throat tightens when he turns to look at me.

"Ah, my little creative genius." His false flattery hurts my ears, but I continue to smile. Neil pulls me next to him. "I was just telling these men that you're docile as they come." He winks at me.

I'm too embarrassed to look over at them. Even with everything I did with Bryan, I never felt shame, but the way Neil says our sex life is tame makes me squirm. I don't like him telling them anything. Appraising eyes move over my body and I know they've read my book. They're wondering if I'd do those things and are picturing me on my knees, naked.

"Neil, where is Maggie?"

"What? She's not back yet?" His tone is off, but he glances around.

My smile falls. "Neil, where is she?"

He smirks. "Well, I know how rambunctious she can be, so I arranged for her to get here after the press leaves."

A bad feelings stirs within me. "Where is she?"

"I told her that you left your purse at her apartment. She went home to grab it."

CHAPTER 3

My heart pounds hard once, and then stops. I can't breathe. I stagger and nearly fall. Neil reaches out for me, grabbing hold of my arm by the elbow. "Hallie, are you all right?"

Suddenly there are people trying to swarm me. They all repeat Neil's words until it sounds like I'm in an empty hallway and there are nothing but echoing voices. I don't blink. Before they can smother me, I shoulder my way past them and race through the house, grabbing my jacket and pulling on my gloves on the way out. It's not winter, but I want them. Part of me knows what's coming, the dark part that says this can't be happening but I'll do anything I need to do to save her.

Neil hurries behind, calling my name, but I'm in the little red car and out of sight before he can stop me.

I floor it and head toward Maggie's, trying to remember exactly where that hellhole of an apartment is located. I'm so mad at Neil that I can't stand it. He shoved the ring on my finger without waiting for an answer. He always does stuff like that, but this is unforgivable.

He didn't know, a voice reminds me. *You never told him how bad Maggie had it.*

At the moment, I don't care. Maggie is in way over her head and I can't let her—

The thought cuts off. I don't want to even consider the rest of the statement. I saw what her boss will do to her if she goes back. I have no idea what I'm going to do when I get there. I'm hoping I'll see her little beat up car racing toward me, but it doesn't happen.

I'm driving down the street, way too fast, and whip into the parking lot. The cherry red sports car means I'm either someone to fear or I'm incredibly stupid. I'm both.

Maggie is the only family I have left. Neil's not the same, and he never will be. I'll be damned if I let some low life drug dealer dump her body in an alley.

I've never been in a fight in my life. I have no idea how to throw a punch or what to do, but that doesn't stop me. Bravery and stupidity seem to be best friends. I wonder which lot I fall into as I race up the staircase and dart down the hall. If she's dead, if he hurt her, I'll kill him. I have no idea how, but he's a dead man.

By the time I get to her door, I'm huffing. I pat the door with my palm and quietly call her name. "Maggie? Maggie are you there?" No answer. I do it again, and again, but she doesn't reply.

My throat tightens and I want to cry, but I don't. Instead, I press my ear to the door and listen. The couple upstairs is quiet tonight. There are no screams, no fighting—no nothing. The soundless halls make my skin prickle. I close my eyes for half a beat when I hear him speak.

"Looking for your friend, pretty girl?"

When I glance up, I'm face to face with Victor Campone.

CHAPTER 4

Victor grins at me in a smug serial-killer way. He hasn't shaved in days so thick dark stubble lines his cheeks. There's a scar along one cheek where hair no longer grows. It's as if someone sliced it open with a pencil and it never healed correctly. The place where skin meets skin is raised and forms a jagged white line that runs over his flesh like a dying river.

I don't value my life, not anymore. I've lost too much and the only person I care about in the world more than myself is on the other side of that door and I'm afraid that I'm not going to like what I see when I go inside. I turn into someone else, someone I don't know, when I answer him my voice is fierce and my gaze is cruel. "Where is she?" I growl like a beast ready to rip his throat out.

I think about what I'll do to him if Maggie's hurt, if he did something to her. I don't fear the repercussions—nothing frightens me at that moment. My heart races faster, but it has nothing to do with this evil man or his cruelty. It's all me. My hands are by my sides, but I'm already picturing them clutching a rusty nail that protrudes from the wall and slamming it into the side of his face, giving him a matching scar down the other cheek.

Victor smirks. Our eyes have been locked this entire time and I don't back down or look away. "Listen, you son of a bitch, I'm not leaving without Maggie."

He appears mildly amused. Victor crosses his meaty arms and leans his shoulder against the wall. "Or you'll do what?"

Evil thoughts flicker behind my eyes in graphic detail, but I reveal none of them. "You don't want to find out." The words come out in a breath.

The man's gaze slips over me once, reevaluating, as if he underestimated me entirely. "Look at you. Well, who would have figured you'd be a tough little shit?" He smiles like he's found a diamond at his feet in this wretched place. He pushes off the wall and reaches into his pocket. I flinch, reaching for mine, like I have a gun or something.

Victor laughs and lifts his palms toward me. "Settle down. I was just grabbing the keys. You can go in and see for yourself." Victor repeats the movement, and my eyes don't stray from his hand. He pulls out a ring with a massive amount of keys attached. They're packed tightly, with little room between each one. The thing must weigh ten pounds. It's amazing his pants didn't fall off.

He steps towards Maggie's door and unlocks it. "Go on. See for yourself."

My heart pounds harder. I don't like this. I don't like him walking behind me or walking into her place like this. I shove aside all rationality and fear, before slamming the door open. The room is empty, just as we left it. Maggie isn't lying in a pool of blood on the floor. Her silent screams aren't trapped in the cracking plaster walls. Then, I spot something different. The rest of the room is exactly as we left it, save one thing—a tiny hole in the window. A spider vein crack travels outward from that hole. Someone shot the window.

I glance down at the floor. There's no blood. Looking up again, I can see straight across into the apartment across the way, the place where the woman was killed last night. When I turn, Victor is right behind me. I slam into him, and he grabs my shirt, before hissing in my face. "I know what you saw and the only reason you're still breathing is that I've lost a rather large investment. Last I saw her, she ran off with you, so now, Miss Raymond—"

His words rattle me and I can't help but ask, "How do you know my name?"

CHAPTER 5

When he grins, I try to pull out of his grip, but he won't release me. I yank so hard, my shirt tears. That awards me with another crooked smirk. I stare at him, without seeing him, as my eyes search the room for a weapon. I'm going to need one, but the only thing I see is that big clunker of a key ring next to the door where he set it down. It's about a foot behind him.

"I have my ways." His voice is cocky and dangerous. He inches closer. "Like it or not, we're in this shit together and your friend has something I need."

"She was supposed to bring you a girl." I utter what Maggie told me last night.

"Yeah, something like that." Victor relaxes a little bit, but he's still trying to turn me into a whimpering, sobbing mess.

I don't cave in. I won't. "So where is she?"

"The fuck if I know. The last person I saw her with was you, this morning while I was taking care of one of my employees who got out of line. I know you saw and the only reason you're still breathing right now is because Maggie is worth more than you, and I intend on you leading me to her. Bring her back here sexy girl, or you'll relive every part of your book with every guy on my payroll. You got it?" He's in my face, snarling.

"I have friends in high places. Be careful who you threaten, Mr. Campone, or you might find yourself on the wrong side of a bad day."

He laughs and pulls away, like I'm hysterical. "There is no one that I can't take, little girl."

"You're wrong. You're clearly forgetting someone important."

Victor smirks and leans back against the kitchen counter. The man is stupid enough to look at the floor, as if I'm no threat. I think he's lying. No, I know he is. Victor knows where Maggie is; he just wants me to leave. The keys are a step away. I pick up the ring and flip through them like I'm examining the shapes. "Yeah, and who's that sweetheart?"

"Me," I move before he can blink, I slam the brass keys into the side of his head. The shot connects with his temple and his eyes flutter once before he goes down. A stream of blood flows from his head like a red ribbon, curling as it travels down his cheek. His eyes close and I wonder if I killed him, but the guy's still breathing.

CHAPTER 6

I take the keys and run to his place across the hall. I thought I'd have to find the right key and can't stop shaking long enough to do anything. That's when the door opens. Maggie peers out from between the jamb. Her green eyes are glistening, like she's been crying.

I rip the door open and a nail tears off. "Maggie!" I lunge for her, but she holds up her hands, preventing me from hugging her.

"Leave, Hallie. Get the fuck out of here before he comes back." Maggie's eye is puffy with a circle darkening around it. One of her wrists is rubbed raw and the other one is bleeding. She's wearing a tattered piece of lingerie that's damp. Her legs have black and blue bruises all over. The bruises are arranged in small clusters of four, like hands gripping too hard made them.

"Maggie." I want to cry. He beat the shit out of her.

"Hallie, go, before he comes back."

I tug on her arm and she stumbles toward the door. "He's not coming back for a little while. Come on. We're gone. Never come back here. Ever."

Maggie digs in her heels. "I can't leave. I'm dead if I leave."

I look her over once. "You're dead if you stay. What the hell happened?"

"I didn't bring him a girl."

"So he used you?" She nods. My lips part as a breath slips out. "Oh, Maggie." Rage is building inside of me. If I had a gun, I'd go back and shoot his nuts off. I don't know exactly what she's doing or what Victor did to her, but I know he beat her and probably raped her. The black and blue marks go all the way up her thighs. Her hair is a mess and her once perfect makeup is smeared across her face like she's been drowning in tears.

Her voice is stern and cold. "It was my choice." Maggie's face glistens with tears and snot. She meets my gaze almost defiantly. "This is my life, not yours."

I stop in my tracks and quit pulling on her. Turning back, I blurt out, "You've done this before?"

"Only when I had to. Hallie, this isn't your problem." Maggie's jaw locks and her once vibrant eyes dart away.

I'm mortified and can't conceal it. I stand there and feel every ounce of grief, regret, and rage ripping from my body. It changes me and I can't stop it. Maggie is the only family I have left. I don't care about Neil, maybe I never did, but people can't live alone. Being alone is a step away from being dead—it's a pace from ending up in a place like this with my face covered in bruises and tears.

There are times in life that creep up slowly, like shadows extending across the earth as the sun sinks below the horizon. Other times it's quick like a breaking twig. My life changes in that moment and I feel it. The walls go up, higher and higher, until there's no one above them, not even God.

I'm alone in my misery, and there is no way I'm letting Maggie go. I'll do what I have to do and the consequences are of little importance.

I snatch her wrist and tug her after me, explaining, "Victor's knocked out in your apartment. We're leaving and never coming back. You're not allowed to leave and you work for me now. This shit is over. It's over, Maggie, and we're never coming back."

Maggie is gasping for air and nearly falls to the floor. "I can't!" She bellows. "Don't make me! Hallie, he'll kill me."

I release her and feel the twisted smirk inch across my lips. I'm not myself, because I'm offering something that I'd never suggest. "Then I'll take care of it. Go to the car."

"Hallie!" Maggie lunges for me, trying to grab my arm.

I round on her. "Go!" Her green eyes meet mine and she knows. She sees the pain has fractured me in two. I'm no longer the same and we both know it. "You'll never see him again." It's a promise.

Maggie nods as she stands there, shivering. She wraps her arms around her middle and looks up at me like we're children again. We stood in this spot before, but last time we didn't fight back. "It'll be all right. It will be." She utters the words more to herself than me. I smile, and holy fuck it practically breaks my face to do it, but I manage. Before she walks down the hall with her clothes in her arms, I touch her shoulder lightly. Maggie nods once at me, then pads down the stairwell and disappears from sight.

My mind is etched with darkness. It's like I've fallen into a pit and can't find my way out. Victor is there, smothering me and if I don't release him, if I don't cast him out, he'll always be there, waiting. Three slow, silent steps back to Maggie's apartment and I see the man still lying on the floor. He's rousing, moaning curses and touching the bloody spot on his temple. Will anyone mourn him? Will someone buy him a tombstone and a cemetery plot? I couldn't afford those things. I couldn't give them to the best man in the world, so why should

Victor Campone have them? He's death incarnate.

Before I know what's happened I'm gripping a dull kitchen knife in my fist, slowly approaching him from behind. Victor sits up and nearly falls to the side. "That fucking bitch." He grips his skull like it's pounding.

This isn't real, is it? My life has come full circle. I'm back at the mercies of the heartless and I refuse to let them rule. I'd rather die, so here I stand. My hand doesn't shake, and the girl I had been vanishes. She's dissolving like an image left in the sun, fading forever until there's no trace remaining.

Victor senses me standing behind him and turns to look over his shoulder. That's when I act. The surprise on his face, the flash of the silver blade on the knife, and the river of blood that runs down his throat like a red river all flash as if they were happening somewhere else. Victor's eyes widen with shock as his hand lifts to his neck and comes away covered in scarlet.

Those eyes, I'll remember the way they looked at me with admiration and anger until I die. His lips part to speak, but I don't care. I drop the knife. It clatters to the floor as I turn on my heel and walk away, leaving Victor dying on the floor.

CHAPTER 7

Time crawls to a stop the same way it did when my father died. Maggie and I drive in silence. I know what we have to do, but I don't want to make her suffer. I tell her what I'm thinking and she agrees. We stop at Target and grab some clearance clothing and change in the car. I take my old clothes, coat, and gloves and put them in the white plastic bag before tossing them in the dumpster behind the store. It's overflowing. They'll come and take away the bloody clothes before morning.

Maggie and I do our make-up in the car. That's when she stops and looks over at me, ready to cry. "They'll find out."

"No, they won't. No one saw us."

"Victor had the place empty so there'd be no one around to hear what he was doing this evening, but his guys don't always leave. What if they saw you?"

I shrug. "Then they can take over and run his drug empire. No one cares about me. He's gone, Maggie. I'm sorry I didn't get there sooner." Our eyes lock and I want to cry, but the tears don't come. Something inside me broke tonight. I know what I have to do, what my life will be like because of this act. I accepted it before I dragged the knife across Victor's throat. I'll sign my contracts, marry Neil, and be the demur wife everyone thinks I am. That will allow me to look after Maggie and make sure this never happens again. Money is power and now I have plenty.

Maggie nods. "So, we go into your party and just pretend that you were offended that the prick didn't invite me?"

"Yup." I smack my lips after reapplying my make-up. "And tease him about not telling me."

"So you grabbed me and went to change?"

"Exactly."

CHAPTER 8

They buy it, even Neil who claims he can spot a liar from fifty feet away. It's all in the eyes, he's told me, the stance, the sweep of the shoulders, and position of the arms. So I do the opposite. I remain poised and smiling. I laugh at his friend's bad jokes and let Cecily tease me about being bitchy about excluding my best friend from the festivities.

I act like I've had too much to drink and poke my finger into her over inflated chest. "If you ever leave her out of any celebration again, you'll be sorry. She's a sister to me." I smile at Maggie who is standing across the room. She's wearing dark tights to cover the bruises on her legs. A thick layer of concealer hides the dark circles under her eyes. She touches the gash on her cheek and goes into a crazy story about how I dared her to slide down the railing on the staircase.

She's laughing. "So, Hallie doesn't think I can do it. Well, screw that. So I get up on the old rail and push off. I was fine until I hit the landing and hurled myself into the wall. It was the funniest thing I've ever done. I thought I'd land on my feet, like on TV."

"And that's why TV isn't real."

"No fuck." She giggles and clicks her glass to the tall, dark, dorky guy standing next to her.

The man gasps like she said the crudest thing he's ever heard, so Maggie turns on the charm. She bats her eyes and touches his arm lightly, laughing into him, like he's the funniest man alive. His demeanor softens and the two of them wander off into the backyard where it's darker.

Cecily and her smoky self is standing next to me. Her boobs are trying to escape from her low cut neckline. "I thought you were having a panic attack or something."

I stare ahead looking at the sea of people, but seeing no one. "Nah, just PMS."

"I'll make sure your friend is invited to every event with you from now on." Cecily clears her throat. "Is there something you want to tell me?" I turn and arch an eyebrow at her while holding a half empty glass of wine in my hand. "Come, come now, you can tell me. Someone with your, let's say tastes, may find one sex boring after a while. It wouldn't surprise anyone to know—"

I take a sip while she's talking and my heart pounds hard. I wonder if I have blood on my face, until she goes into that last sentence. I nearly choke on my Merlot and set the glass down, hushing her. "No, of course not!"

"Because if you were gay, it wouldn't be a big deal." She blows smoke in my face.

Grabbing her arm, I steer Cecily away from the massive amount of ears and over to the hallway. "No! I'm not gay and if you give Neil that impression I swear to God—"

She offers an amused grin and touches my forearm. "Come on now, Hallie. I didn't mean anything by it. You two are close and it would make sense, with your background and hers."

"Yeah, well, you're off base here and the man who just stuck this ring on my finger will have a stroke if you even mention the idea." Neil has his natural order philosophy and that would scare him off. I need him to stay. He can't leave, and a suggestion like this will send him running the other way.

She raises her pink claws and smiles. "Oh, I won't, but if you ever need someone to confide in, I'm here. That's all I wanted to offer. I won't judge." Her old eyes hold mine for a moment. She can sense the secret buried deep within me, but there's more than one. So even if she discovers Bryan, she'll never know what I did tonight.

Being defensive is making her think that there's something to defend, so I lean in close and say, "Listen, I'd tell you if that were the case. I know I can trust you," When did I get so good at lying? "But Neil is weird with stuff like that. He's okay with my book since it wasn't real, you know? It's not like that stuff is part of our life. You do understand, don't you?"

She understands all right. Cecily nods slowly and I know I'm fucked. She knows there's a story there, another lover. Fine. It's better than knowing I just slashed the throat of Victor Campone.

CHAPTER 9

Maggie stays with Neil and me for a few days. It's strangely silent because Neil and Maggie usually fight like the world's going to end and one of them will have the final say. But the bickering has ceased and only quietness hangs in the air. Bryan hasn't been around and Jon never tried to collect on his money. I was able to get Cecily to advance me five grand, because she thought that was plenty. I don't tell anyone that I have it and keep my thoughts close to my heart—or what's left of it—as I devise an escape plan.

Good people would be ridden with grief and question their very existence for taking a life, but I don't. I hate to think of the meaning behind my lack of empathy. A life is a life. At one time, I thought every breathing thing held value and I had no right to destroy it. Now I have blood on my hands, and it will never wash away. They're stained with sin that goes bone deep and I don't even care.

I can't discuss it with Maggie. She'll flip out. And if I tell Neil, knowing him, he'll call the cops, so I keep my thoughts to myself. Cecily comes around more and more often, and acts like the mother I never had. Her behavior disgusts me. There's no room in my life for another mother. One was plenty. Once in a while when I go to sleep, I can hear my mother's voice and that giggle that said she was gone, too stoned to care. I'd stay locked in that tiny closet until she remembered to let me out. Maggie wasn't so lucky. Her stepfather never forgot her and used her until her little body collapsed.

I don't know how she endured such things, but then again, she says the same thing back to me. She acts like my mother was a monster. Mom was no saint, but she kept me clothed most days and out of sight.

She could have sold me, but she didn't. It's not that my mom brings me the warm fuzzies. No, it's more that things could have been worse. She could have traded a hit for my young body, but she didn't.

Meanwhile, the man who was supposed to protect Maggie was ravaging her instead. I bet anything that she was reliving those nights when Victor had hold of her. Although Maggie won't talk about it, her posture speaks volumes. She's sitting sideways in a chair, with her knees tucked into her chest, and her arms folded over her ankles. That's when the doorbell rings.

I walk over and pat her shoulder, thinking it's the pizza guy, but when I yank the door open, Bryan Ferro is standing there with that smug grin on his face. Without a word, I slam the door shut.

Maggie laughs. "You're going to pay for that."

"Like I care." I pad across the room and sit on the couch just before Bryan cracks open the door. I haven't seen him in a few days. His pallor looks vibrant again and there's no sleepiness in his eyes.

"Nice manners, Hallie. Real nice." Bryan scoffs and steps into the room, closing the door behind him.

I shrug. "It's about what you deserve."

"Since when do we get what we deserve? Because if that's the case, I'd like to file a complaint." That sexy grin lines his lips and I wish things weren't so tense between us.

"What are you doing here, Bryan?"

He glances around the room. "Is Neil here?"

I nod. "Yeah, in the kitchen. He tries to avoid Maggie." Maggie smirks and wiggles the tips of her fingers at him.

"Well, then he won't mind if I claim my prize now, would he?"

Maggie's jaw drops. "You're going to nail her, here, where Neil can see?"

Bryan actually has the audacity to laugh, which makes Neil come from the kitchen. "I don't care if he watches, but that wasn't my intention. I want you here and now. I have an appointment later and I was thinking that with all this blackmail, there's been very little sex. I intend on fixing that." Bryan glances at Neil. "Hope you don't mind if I borrow her for a little bit."

I don't offer consent. I say nothing, but I can plainly see the nukes going off behind Neil's eyes. Bryan intends to fuck me in Neil's bed. "Very smooth," I offer and shake my head.

"You disapprove?" Bryan asks, sounding shocked.

"It doesn't matter, does it?" We walk into the master bedroom and Bryan grins broadly. Neil says nothing, and after a few moments, I hear his car start. The tires squeal as he drives down the street. Bryan grins and leans against the wall with his hands behind his hips. "Well, come on. Take it all off, Hallie. I want to see every inch of you."

I do as he asks, cold and lifeless. He notices the fear is gone and that there's no hesitation. When I'm completely nude, he pats Neil's bed and asks me to sit by him. "What's wrong?"

Shaking my head, I reply, "No. The deal was for my body, not my mind. And even if I wanted to, I can't talk about it."

"Then, maybe I can help you forget."

"Fine, do anything you want. Anything…" The word hangs between us as my heart pounds hard. I need to be dominated and controlled right now. I need to stop thinking, if only for a moment. I know Bryan can do that, and I want him to.

Bryan pushes his hair out of his face, revealing a softness to him that makes him seem vulnerable even though I know he's not. "What would my Hallie like tonight? Maybe I should come here, or here," his finger touches my lips as he grins. "Or are you up for something more adventurous?"

I lean in and whisper, "Anything. Just get my mind off of everything else. I don't want to think for a while."

Bryan steps toward me. "Sounds perfect. No questions. No answers. And I won't hold back." I can't speak of what I've done or why I need this now. Neil would never approve, but Bryan's here and willing. I no longer love. The part of my heart that holds compassion and reverence is dead.

Lips parted, I say nothing. I just nod, and feel my nipples harden. The look he's giving me brings back old times and I want to get lost in the past. I want to forget my life and everything in it. I want him. I need him and my body responds, aching for memories from long ago.

Bryan reaches for me and whispers in my ear. "I'll come inside you, deep between your legs and if there's any left over, I'll cover your breasts with it and lick them until you're spotless. Forget yourself Hallie. Let go, let it all go."

I put my hands on his chest, sliding off his dark leather jacket, followed by his shirt. Bryan swallows hard, and tugs me toward him, pulling me by the waist. His lips hover above mine, hesitantly. I know he's thinking of the way things were before—about the things that drove us apart—and that fight. Without another word his lips come crashing down on mine. It's a desperate kiss as his tongue forces its way into my mouth. He licks me, stroking my mouth as he kisses me, tasting me. Bryan presses me to the wall showing me how much he wants me. He's so hard that every inch of his long, beautiful shaft presses firmly against my stomach, and I want him inside me.

What does that make me? A whore? A person bent on living in the past? I'm engaged to Neil and I'm fucking my blackmailer in Neil's bed without remorse. I want him so badly that I'm ashamed of it.

Breathless, he pulls away, "How badly do you want me Hallie?" He asks the question as if he can read my mind.

I answer by taking his hand and pressing it to my slick skin. His eyes are on me, watching, as I slip his hand down my body and between my legs. Holding me there for a moment, Bryan strokes the small, sensitive flesh and breathes in deeply. I savor his scent and the way he feels against me. As he gazes at me, I spread my legs and look at him.

Caution flashes in Bryan's eyes, but quickly vanishes. He wonders what came over me, what made me change. The last few times, I held back, but not now. I know he wants to ask, but won't.

Bryan leans his forehead against mine. "You've always been my wet dream, Hallie," he whispers. His eyes move around the room. It's nothing special. Neil is boring. It could double as a generic hotel room anywhere in the United States. Bland colors, dark headboard, and a chair.

Bryan grabs my wrist hard and pulls me toward the chair. "Feet apart."

I do as he says. The tone of his voice is perfectly domineering. He takes his belt, and snaps it. I flinch, wondering if he's going to strike me, but he says, "Hands behind your back."

I move my hands and he places the belt around my wrists, using it to hold my arms back. When he's done, he steps away and looks at me standing by the chair, his eyes slipping hungrily over my curves. His gaze lingers on the patch of hair between my legs. He kneels in front of me, and slowly slides his hands up the back of my thighs, pressing his face into the V between my legs as he does it. When his hands move over the swell of my hips, he inhales deeply, and his fingers press against my skin.

I step back, my back and my calves bumping the chair. My feet start to move back together, attempting to clench the warmth building between my thighs, but he swats me and says, "Come here."

With a grin on his face, he unties the belt and forms a loop before dragging me over to the closet door. Bryan makes a slipknot at one end that holds my wrists and closes the belt in the top of the door. My arms are pinned above my head. I loved it when he did this, but it was long ago.

Bryan unbuttons and slowly slides down the zipper. He keeps the dark pants on, and pulls out his long, thick erection. He hesitates, stopping before me, holding it in his hand. I know he's questioning himself. The conflict spreads across his face.

"Do it," I plead, hanging my head back and letting my hair trail down to my waist. I know his eyes are on me, watching my body move in front of him, tied up and ready to take. I'm breathing hard, wanting him to do it. When a moment passes, I look at him and say, "Take me right now and make me yours in every way possible. Do it."

"I don't want to hurt you," he says, his eyes on mine.

"Then don't," I breathe. "You're the one in control here. Make me writhe. Make me scream. Take me the way you want to. But, Bryan—"

"Yeah?"

"I like things a little rough, more so than before."   After I say it, my lips remain parted and I take a deep breath. My chest swells, forcing my nipples toward him. The door presses against my back and I lean into it wondering what he'll do.

CHAPTER 10

Bryan takes my face in his hands. "If you don't like it, tell me." I nod slowly, his warm hands still holding my cheeks.

It's like someone flipped a switch. Bryan's eyes grow darker, more carnal. He releases my face and presses his toned body against me. Pushing my back into the door, he makes sure I can feel every inch of him. He pulls out a silver chain with tweezers on each end and attaches them to my nipples. I gasp as he tightens them. The weight of the chain tugs, making me bite my lip. When he presses into me, the chains go taught and pull gently as he slides over my body. A small gasp escapes between my lips. Bryan watches me, his green eyes locked on mine.

He takes one finger and places it on my pink lips, while his other hand slides lower past my belly and between my legs. I gasp. He moves quickly, feeling my sensitive nub with his thumb, smoothing his finger over the silk flesh, and watching my face as he does it.

My chin lifts as I try not to moan. I fight the sensations that are erupting inside of me, the feelings he's creating. His fingers move on top of my clit, while he tugs the chain gently. He feels me growing wetter and then, without warning—without a change in expression—he thrusts his finger inside of me. He's still for a moment, watching my eyes. I blink slowly, feeling him there between my legs.

Bryan pushes his finger harder, deeper as he watches me. His breath washes over my lips making me feel lightheaded. When he pulls his finger out, he lifts it to my mouth. Outlining my lips, he watches me, spreading my damp heat like lipstick. I blink slowly, heart pounding, and aroused beyond comprehension.

"Taste," he breathes and pushes his finger into my mouth. I flick my tongue against his finger, but he holds it there and says, "Suck the come off my finger, Hallie." I hesitate, but he says, "Do it." My tongue wraps around his finger, sucking it, tasting what he tastes.   His eyes are burning, watching me.

As I suck his finger, he lowers his other hand between my legs, parting my smooth skin. Sensations explode inside of me, but before I can savor them, the feeling changes. Bryan's hard length slams into me, making me suck his finger harder. He pulls his finger out of my mouth, and wraps his hands around my waist. He remains still for a moment, breathing fast and hard. Then he pulls out slowly and thrusts back in, slamming me into the door. My knees tremble as he slowly drives me crazy. I want more. I want him to manhandle me and make me drunk with passion. Wipe away my fear with lust, erase my memory for just a moment, and take all the pain that's flooding me with it.

I just want to feel him and nothing else. The world fades away until I don't know how much time has passed. My arms ache as he uses me, pushing into me over and over again. My head hangs to the side and then tips back. I gasp every time and my breasts shake with the force of his thrusting.

Something uncoils inside of me. I want his hands on me, doing everything at once. Delicate strands of passion erupt inside of me, sending tingles down my thighs and breasts. Every place I want him to touch sizzles like a live current. Arching my back, I press my hips into him, only to get slammed back.

His thrusts change to teases, gently pushing in and pulling out. He's so hard, so perfect. I want to wrap my legs around his hips, but I can't. Jagged breaths consume me and the room is beyond hot. My body is dripping with sweat. Tilting my head back, I look up at the ceiling. That's when his hands find my breasts. My lips form an O, but I say nothing. He feels the softness, the fullness of my curves as he pushes his long, hard length into me slowly, torturing me, over and over again.

Taking my nipples between his fingers, he twists them gently and tightens the clamps. I cry out, thrusting my breasts to him, but the pole stops me. Gasping, I can barely breathe.

He grins, "Shhh. No sounds from you. I want this between us."

I don't understand. Then why did he parade in past Neil and Maggie? At that moment, I don't care. I do as he says and bite my lip to remain silent. He slams deep into my core again, and my mouth flies open. I swallow the sound before he hears it. The only noise is a rush of air being forced out of my lungs.

"Good girl," he purrs and pulls out before thrusting back in, deeper this time. The tone of his voice makes me melt.

Before I can think another thing, Bryan's fingers clamp around the nipple chains. His hips stay pressed flush to mine, his length lost inside of me. My jaw falls open, and I see him watching me, waiting for me to make a noise. My eyes lock on his, while white-hot sensations swirl through my body, building tighter and higher. He slowly adds more pressure, teasing and pulling my nipples tighter and longer, making the tweezers tighter and tighter. The heat in my stomach sears through my body. I shift my hips and try to rock against him, but he stills me.

"No, no. Not yet."

I gasp, "I like to be spanked."

"Really?" I nod. His hand comes down hard on my ass. Both cheeks sting. He does it while he's still in me, which makes me clench and tighten around him. He gasps and does it again, and again. The impact of his hands feels so good. The warm sting sends shudders through me in waves that don't die down. They travel through my lower stomach and spread through my entire body. Every delicious tingle courses through me, making me slide my tongue over my teeth. I do it without thinking. It's a reaction to him, to what he's doing to me.

Without warning, Bryan pulls out. It makes me crazy. My hips buck, but I can't reach him. The belt cuts into my wrists as I pull against my restraints. I pant, watching him as he moves away from me. Lust is burning through my body. I can't control myself. Pulling my wrists hard, I try to break free from the belt again, but I can't. It just digs in tighter.

He grins, watching me struggle, until I stop and look up at him. The expression on his face, the intensity of his eyes, makes my stomach flip. My breath hitches in my throat as Bryan steps close enough to touch me, but he doesn't. I'm panting. My eyes are begging him to do something—to make me come, to let me fuck him—anything.

"Tell me what you want, Hallie. Beg me for it," he breathes the words next to my ear. The reaction within me is quick and violent. His warm breath makes my clit throb and it feels like I'll die if he doesn't touch me, if he doesn't finish what he started. He stands so close, nearly touching me, but doesn't slide his fingers down my waist. He doesn't touch my breast and doesn't tease my nipples. It makes me want him even more. I feel like a chained animal, unable to think. "Answer me beautiful woman," he commands and I feel the sting of his hand on my ass.

My body is so tightly coiled that the slap makes me moan. I didn't expect it, but before I could bite back my sounds, they flew past my lips. I gasp, shocked that I wasn't able to muffle the noise or stop it in time. Bryan's hand flies a second time, harder. He watches my face as I wince under his hand. The sting is quick, and I know that I'm going to have a problem walking later, but I don't care. I cry out, saying his name, thrusting my breasts toward him.

A wicked look twists his lips into a sexy smile, "Answer me." His voice sounds like a growl and when I can't do anything but pant uncontrollably, his hand lands a third time. But he doesn't release me. Instead he grabs my cheek in his hand and squeezes. The sting intensifies from the way he grabs me. Bryan's beautiful body is covered in a thin sheen of sweat, as he handles me roughly. "Tell me what you want."

My voice is a breath. Every desire races out in a rush, "I want your hands on me, in me. I want you to fuck me senseless. Fuck me, Bryan."

"Beg for it, Hallie. Beg louder," his grip tightens on my ass making my body press into his. A beads of sweat roll down my spine.

My voice quivers as I beg, no longer capable of maintaining any ounce of restraint. "Please, Bryan—please! Fuck me. Fuck my pussy. Fill me with come. Please baby. Please…" I continue to beg him, as his hands slide over my hips and down between my legs. When he touches my clit, I moan. Bryan leans his head back, watching me. "Fuck me, baby. Please." My hips buck into his hand. In response, he tightens his fingers on my clit. I cry out, "Fuck me! Please! Bryan! I need you! Please!"

When I say his name, he shatters. Before I know what happens, his hands are holding my wrists over my head as his hard length slams into me over and over again. He thrusts harder and deeper each time with his hands slipping down my arms. Slamming himself harder and harder into me, he watches my breasts sway and bounce until he takes both in his hands and pinches my nipples hard. I scream out, but it only makes him pinch harder, until the chain falls free. It falls at my feet and he leaves it there.

Bryan moves, pushing into me faster and faster. The heat between my legs is coursing through my body. It feels like I can't be tamed. There isn't enough of him to ever satisfy me, ever. When his fingers clamp harder on my sore nipples, my eyes fly open. He looks me in the eye as he thrusts into me once—hard. My back hits the door and he holds me there, watching me. Lips parted, he breathes saying nothing. His hands gently push the hair back from my eyes. He stills for a moment and I can't stand it. His dick is in me but no matter how much I wiggle, I can't get him to fuck me.

With his entire body, he flattens me against the door. His eyes burn with lust, his brow drips with sweat. "Come for me, baby," he breathes and pounds into me fast and furious. He doesn't stop when I scream. He keeps pounding against me until my body can't wind any tighter.

Each time he sinks into me I feel higher and higher. I can't breathe, but I don't want him to stop. His body crushes me, as he rides me, rocking into me furiously. I moan, and can tell how hard he's pushing, how much I'm going to hurt later, but I don't care. In the moment, it feels so good. My skin tingles and is dripping with sweat. My breasts bounce harder and higher with every slam of his body against mine. And without another thought, I come. My scream rips through my throat. I can't come quietly, not when he does this. Bryan pounds me harder as the delicious swirling sensations erupt throughout my body. I feel him push into me hard and deep, and he comes a few moments later.

Spent, I hang from the door shivering, ready to fall to the floor. Bryan pulls away and looks me over. Lips parted, he just stares at me for a moment before undoing the belt. When my hands fall to my sides, my arms burn. Bryan takes me in his arms and carries me to the bed. He sits me down in front of him and rubs out the sore muscles in my arms and shoulders. My head droops to the side as he does it. Every inch of me is tingling. I don't want the moment to end, but Bryan stops.

I turn and look at him. He's glowing, covered in a thin layer of sweat that smells so good. I want to lick it off, but I just nod. He turns his emerald eyes away and says, "I guess I should get going."

"You're leaving?" Suddenly, I feel very naked. I pull the throw blanket off the bed and wrap it around my shoulders.

"Yeah, unless you want me to stay and tell Neil all about how I nailed his fiancée." He watches me for a second. His brow is covered in sweat and his face is glistening. "What's wrong?" He could always read me so well. I want to tell him about Victor, but I can't.

I say something else. "Neil proposed and I said yes." I hold up my ring.

"Yeah, saw that. You really agreed?" Bryan sits next to me.

"Not really. He agreed for me." We're both quiet for too long.

Bryan dresses and says, "I'll be back to have my way with you again soon. Next time your asshole fiancée better have you ready for me. And I want you to wear these when you're with me and only me." He lifts the chain from the floor and tosses it to me.

The bedroom door flies open and Neil is livid. He glances at me and back at Bryan, "You think this is funny?"

"No, I think she needs something you can't give her. I'm giving you a single chance to break your agreement and fuck your fiancée. But you have to do it like an animal. Satisfy her."

Neil's face scrunches in disgust. "I do satisfy her and without this barbaric behavior. Making love does not have a place for gagging, tying or oppressing women in any way. I'm sure Hallie just took one for the team, you deranged piece of shit."

That was the crudest thing I've ever heard Neil say and I want to laugh, because it's pathetically weak. The man who's using me offered to break his agreement if Neil promised to nail me and have monkey sex. The man should have said yes, but he stood by his morals and said no. I'm too tired to think of what that means. What just happened here?

"She'll be taking more than one hit for the team." Bryan winks. "I'll see you tomorrow, sex slave. I have a collar for you and you're going to wear it." Bryan shakes Neil's hand. "You're a smart man. What are a few months of infidelity compared to a life time of riches, right?"

Neil tightens his jaw. "So you plan for this to continue for a few months?"

"Probably not that long. I get bored fucking the same woman day in and day out. No worries, Neil. She's your mess, not mine." With that, Bryan turns on his heel and leaves.

"Neil," I'm ready to burst into tears. The judgment is strewn across his face. "Hallie, this isn't natural. You're not a wild animal. Does he get his kicks pretending you are?"

I shrug. I don't want to talk about it. "I have no idea."

"Am I supposed to let him bang you in my bed, whenever he wants?"

I stare straight ahead waling. "Until he grows tired of me, yes. Deal with it. You're the one who told me to do it." I snap the last sentence. "And he just gave you a way out. You didn't take it." I stare at him, and tug the blanket tighter around my shoulders.

Neil rolls his eyes. "I thought it was one night."

"So did I. We were wrong about a lot of things."

CHAPTER 11

I should feel embarrassed, but I don't. The next day I sit with Maggie on the couch while Neil is out. She's been very quiet since I picked her up from her old place. Maggie stares into space, and I know that memory is tangling with the new one and playing over and over again in her mind.

"Do you want to talk about it?" I ask, already knowing the answer.

She inhales and shakes her head, before offering me a forced smile. "There's nothing to say. Same old shit. Nothing's changed, but it hurts more now." She smiles like something's funny. "I would have thought it hurt more when I was a kid. Guess not."

"What'd he do?"

"The same old stuff. Victor likes to own things." She shifts in her seat and then stands, putting distance between us. "I was supposed to set him up with a girl. He has a type, round hips, dark hair, and pale skin—like Nicole Kidman—but a brunette. So every week, I bring him someone. They get a few hundred and he does what he does. On weeks that I can't find anyone, I sub, but this time." She stops speaking and shakes her head. "I shouldn't have. It's usually just rough sex. He slaps me around and nails me. I go home and that's that. But this time…" She shakes her head and looks over her shoulder at me. "I don't want to talk about it. I tried to get away and then gave up when he said what he'd do to me, and then to you. He slapped me around for a while, taking me however he wanted, and then I heard your voice and was scared to death that he'd get you too. I'm so sorry, Hallie."

"It's not your fault." I feel horrible that I let her life crumble like this. We were supposed to be there for each other. "I should have gotten there sooner. I would have. I wish I could take it all back."

Maggie smiles sadly and wraps her arms around her middle. "Yeah, me too. So now what? No offense, but I can't stand Neil."

I nod. "I was thinking that I should get a place of my own before the wedding. It'll be me and you."

Maggie's gaze sweeps the floor. "You're seriously going to marry him?" I nod and give her a look that says don't press it right now. She adds, "I'd love to, but you know I can't afford to do it."

"Yes, you can. I got part of my advance. We can go house hunting whenever you want, oh, and this part isn't optional—you work for me now. I'm going to need a personal assistant to tell me what to do, you know, someone a little bossy."

Maggie giggles and shoves me, then slaps her hands over her mouth, and repeats the action. "No way!"

"Way." It's so good to see a burst of happiness flash in her eyes for a brief moment. But as soon as she blinks, it's gone, lost within the depths of agony that fill her soul.

One day she'll stop fighting back. One day she'll give in, give up.

She would have already if I hadn't shown up. Some people take you straight to Hell. It's ironic, because I have blood on my hands and it doesn't feel like she's pulling me down. It's more like I'm pulling Maggie up from the torturous life she's known, and hidden with that pretty smile.

I don't regret my actions. The thought makes my skin tingle. In the back of my mind, I wonder what kind of person that makes me, but I straighten my spine and get up. It makes me who I am and there's nothing more to consider. I did what I had to do. I wouldn't have touched Victor if he left her alone, if he hadn't threatened to come after us, but he did. I saw the fear in Maggie's eyes and the truth. If Victor Campone had lived, we would have died.

"You hungry?" I ask as I pad toward the fridge.

"Yeah, a little bit." Maggie has been sitting with her feet curled under her butt and looking at her hands since I picked her up at Victor's. She rarely makes eye contact. I think the fight was knocked out of her. It shows up in spurts, but it's like a car that's running out of gas. I'm so worried about her. After everything she's been through…

This can't be what undoes her. It can't.

Because it's my fault this time.

Every other time, Maggie fought back. She never gave up, never gave in, and now my best friend is slumped on the couch, covered in bruises and cuts, with eyes that resemble black holes—they suck everything in, but see nothing. They feel nothing, not anymore.

I smile and say something stupid, trying to make her laugh, but I don't even get a pity grin. After tugging the fridge door open, I groan aloud. Neil is working today and failed to go shopping.

Maggie asks, "What'd he do?"

"He took all the leftovers from the party to work. I thought it was fine because he's supposed to go shopping, but he didn't." I'm leaning into the empty fridge staring at a carton of expired milk and a jar of pickles. I'm not eating that. I slam the fridge and add, "I'll run out. Does Chinese sound good?"

Maggie usually protests and offers to pay for stuff, but today she just nods. "Great!" I say, sounding chipper. She'll come back around. She will. If I keep telling myself that it'll happen right? I suddenly realize if she doesn't rebound, killing Victor wasn't enough revenge to get even for what he did to Maggie.

CHAPTER 12

I grab my keys and start the engine. The cherry red car purrs as I pull out of the driveway and zip to the take-out place. When I'm about to pull into the parking lot, a cop pulls up behind me, with his red lights flashing. I wasn't speeding. Damn. It must be true that red cars get pulled over more than any other color.

I pull over and throw the car into park, careful to keep my hands on the steering wheel. Dad told me to never go for my purse or glove box until the cop was standing by the car. The guy's got to see my hands or he might shoot me, well that's not exactly the way Dad said it, but it's what he meant.

I push the button on the window just as the cop walks over. He's wearing that dark uniform that makes me want to run screaming into my room and hide under my bed.

He's not that guy. Stop it, Hallie, I scold myself, but it doesn't help. By now, my hands are shaking.

"License and registration, please." The guy is late thirties, and kind of scary looking. By scary, I mean it looks like he could take my little body and fold it accordion style and shove it in his trunk. The guy is all lean muscle and he looks pissed off. I can't imagine what I've done.

I reach for the glove box to pull out the papers Jon mentioned, but all I can find is the book about the car and the last oil change notice. No papers. No registration. My heart lurches. Fuck. I start thinking that Jon played me, but even he isn't that low. And the cop hasn't asked me to step out of the car or anything. My taillight is out or something, that's all. This is nothing.

I dig through my purse and manage to pull out my little wallet. My face turns ashen when I see the empty slot where my driver's license should have been. I glance over at the policeman and say softly, "It's gone."

"You don't have a license or registration on this vehicle?" He says something into his shoulder after hearing a buzz in his earpiece. "Step out of the car, ma'am."

I'm shaking now. "I didn't do anything wrong. Someone took my license. I have one."

He ignores me and backs me into the hood. His sunglasses come off. When he tucks them away, he asks, "Do you know you're driving a stolen vehicle?"

"It's not stolen."

"Oh?"

I shake my head, ready to cry. Jon wouldn't do this to me, he wouldn't. "Jonathan Ferro sold me this car a couple of days ago for ten thousand dollars. I haven't had a chance to file the paperwork yet. I thought I had a few days?"

The cop nods. He turns me to face the hood and pats me down. "Nice story. The car is worth a lot more than that. If you're going to lie at least make the story sound convincing."

"It's true! Jon sold it to me for ten grand. Ask him! I'm not lying."

I feel cold metal bite into my wrists as handcuffs slip around my arms. I start to panic. My heart races too fast and the world becomes a blur. I can't stop talking, pleading, and as the cop shoves me in the back of his car the whole awful event replays in vivid detail in my mind.

I close my eyes and try to shut it out, but the colors brighten and the sounds from over a decade ago ring loudly in my ears as tears streak down my cheeks. The past and the present slam together with such violence that I can't stand it.

My mother swears at me before shoving me in the closet. Little hands wrap around me, and I know my baby brother, Anthony, is terrified. He's grown so thin that his bones feel sharp under my palms. He cries until he goes silent, until he falls asleep, until my mother has had her fill of drugs and lovers. I hear her laugh. I could never make her happy like that. I hear the sounds of sex, until something changes. The normal party isn't normal anymore.

The policeman that pulled me from the closet tried to take my brother's lifeless body from my arms. I didn't understand. I protected him from her. I watched out for Anthony, but after everything I did, it wasn't enough. They thought I killed him at first. They shoved me into the back of the car and I screamed at them until I couldn't cry anymore. I wanted my brother, but they said he was dead.

I didn't believe them.

Now, I have trouble believing anyone and this cop has opened a wound that is so deep it cuts me to the bone. No, it wasn't the cop—it was Jon.

I can't help the shivering, but I don't cry. They book me and ask me questions that I've heard before. The paint never changes in places like this. The people are the same. The smell is identical. I stare blankly, trying to keep my mind in one piece, but I feel it cracking bit by bit.

Who will save Maggie? If I lose it, who's there for her? *No one. Pull it together, Hallie.*

I get one call, so I call the person they're trying to keep me away from, the man who's blackmailing me for sex.

When he answers the phone, Bryan sounds weary. I don't know how else to put it. I would have thought he was sleeping, but there's something in his voice that tells me he hasn't slept in a long time. "Suffolk County PD. Let me guess, is this Jon or Trystan?"

"Neither," my voice is so small, so mousey that it barely makes a sound.

I hear him shift and Bryan sounds more alert when he replies, "Hallie?"

"Come get me. I'll owe you. Anything you want, just come get me." I hand the phone back to the officer at the desk and am led back to my cell.

CHAPTER 13

I'm sitting across from a woman who can't stop weeping. She goes on and on about unpaid parking tickets and that she'll lose her job for this, but she didn't make enough to pay the tickets. She starts to hyperventilate and mentions medicine. That's the only time the officer outside the bars looks over at her. They remove her from my cell, saying they'll get her meds.

Someone else comes in and sits next to me. Her face is bruised on one side. "Hey."

I stare at her and say nothing. My arms are folded across my chest and I'm leaning against the wall thinking of ways to castrate Jon Ferro. He knew my past and what this would do to me.

The woman is no more than a girl, barely eighteen, with big round eyes and baby fat on her cheeks. Her face doesn't have that angular look that comes around twenty-two years old. Her dark hair is long and in a messy ponytail.

She sighs and rests her back against the cold cement wall. "Are you in for the night? I hope I am. He needs time to cool off. The only bad part is the lice soap, but the rest is okay. Plus it'll give him time. I can't be around him when he's like this. He's usually great, but on nights like this one, I'm better off staying here. I'm not making my call. Hey, you look familiar." She talks without taking a breath and stares at me the entire time.

"We've never met," is all I say.

She nods and continues, releasing a tidal wave of words. I sit and listen to her life, to her story, and feel nothing but pity. She's like Maggie and me. She has no one that cares, no one to listen to her voice and find solace in her touch.

I don't know how long I've been there but by the time they call my name, the young woman was taken for a shower and lead to her cell for the night. Imagine wishing for a cell instead of going home. It makes me want to cry, and there's not a fucking thing I can do about it. I can't even take care of myself.

The cell door slides open and makes the most god-awful sound. "Hallie Raymond, collect your things at the front desk and go home with the friend who paid your bail. If you screw up, he's going to be the one who pays for it, so best behavior."

I nod and make my way to the front desk. It feels like I haven't blinked for ages, but I do when I see Bryan. As I walk up behind him I notice the way he breathes, the way his shoulders hunch forward like he's being guarded—or in pain. I stop behind him and watch for a moment. His hips are narrow as always, he hasn't lost much weight, but his hair doesn't shine the way it used to. His breaths are shallow and short, like he's been running. A horrible feeling drips down my spine as I stare at him.

At that moment, Bryan feels my eyes on him and turns. He has that playful grin on his face. "If you wanted to wear cuffs, I

have some. I would have been happy to—
oof!" I crash into him with the full force of
my body and hold him tight.

Bryan is shocked at first. His arms take a
moment to close around me, and after they
do, he holds me. I feel his voice, the warm
stirring of breath, as he whispers in my ear,
"Let's get out of here." He releases me and
I nod. That's when he tells me the last thing
I want to hear. "There are reporters out
front."

"What?" My jaw drops in horror.

"I've made arrangements to leave
through the back, but there will be
someone. There always is. Everyone is
going to know what happened by
morning." Bryan takes my hand and leads
me after an officer that ushers us through a
room with filing cabinets and out the back
of the police station to a black Hummer.
I'm shoved inside, but not before a flash
goes off and I looked straight into the
camera.

Bryan shoves him back, but the shot was
already taken. He climbs in after me and
says, "Drive."

"I'm not your fucking chauffeur, Bryan. Say please." A guy about my age, with dark hair that hangs in his face, is in the driver's seat. Oversized sunglasses obscure his eyes.

"Fuck you, Trystan."

Trystan rolls his eyes and pulls away in his oversized, environmentally irresponsible machine, aiming at stray reporters, as he exists the parking lot. "People would be nicer to you if you were nicer to them. That's all I'm saying." Trystan is quiet but I feel his eyes on me. When I look up he answers what I was thinking about. "Jon didn't do this to you."

Slowly, my chin tips up and our eyes meet in the review mirror. "Jon Ferro is a dead man. He knows what this did to me. It was the worst thing he could have done."

Bryan takes my hand and weaves our fingers together. "It wasn't Jon. Please wait to kill him until tomorrow."

"I could kill him now. Bryan, I took care of Campone and I can take care of anyone that messes with Maggie or me. I'm not a child anymore," I hiccup and shiver as the past and present slam together again. My brother starved to death. He died in my arms and I was too dumb and small to know any better. I say I was an only child because it's easier than telling people that story, but the Ferros know everything. They're like roaches that can seek out every lie in every dark corner of your soul. "I won't be decimated by Jon. Fuck him."

Trystan and Bryan exchange a look, but no one says anything. Bryan pulls me into his arms and holds me until we pull up in front of an ancient motel. Gross is the best way to describe it. I bet they rent rooms by the hour. Trystan tosses Bryan the room key. "Stay put until I find out what happened. I think I already know, although the details are sketchy."

I shake my head, "No, I can't. Maggie is back there and she needs me. And Neil—"

Bryan sighs, running his hands through his hair. After he does it, he shakes his hand by his side. "Maggie will be all right. And Neil is a douche. Besides, he knows I took you for the night. Apparently you told Maggie I was blackmailing you because she tried to nail me in the temple with her heel." That makes me smile. "Oh, you think that's funny?" Bryan tickles me and leans in close. Those green eyes sparkle for a moment before the haze returns. "Come on Raymond. I plan on using you until you forget who you are."

CHAPTER 14

I'm breathless by the time I feel him shudder within me. Bryan is naked and covered in a slick sheen of sweat. My legs are tightly gripping his hips as he pounds into me over and over again. He repeats the rocking motion until I scream out his name, and then he falls on top of me. Breathing hard, he rolls to the side with a smile on his face. He pushes his dark damp hair out of his face and watches me. "I've never had so much fun breaking the law in my entire life."

"Oh? And just how many women have you blackmailed, Mr. Ferro?" I prop myself up on my side and debate pulling the blanket up, so I opt for the sheet, but Bryan stops me.

His hand is on mine and he keeps it there until I drop the linens. "No clothes, no sheets, no blankets, nothing. You're my naked slave tonight. I want to see you." His eyes dip to my breasts and slowly slip up my neck and back to my eyes.

"Nice dodge."

"You don't really want me to answer that, do you?" He grins and places his hands behind his head. God, his body is beautiful, toned and perfect. I wonder how many pills he's taken tonight, how high he is right now and what he'll remember tomorrow. I want him to remember me— every bit of every moment. "If I have done this before, then I'm a total dick, but if I haven't, then you'll know I'm into you. Since you're engaged to someone else, though, I don't see how this goes well, either way. Let's pretend you didn't ask."

He has a point. Licking my lips, I ask, "You don't mind Neil? And the engagement thing?"

He shakes his head. "Nah, this is temporary."

My heart sinks a little bit. I ask the question that's been floating in my head since this started. "Then, when will it end? Before my wedding or after? Before my bridal shower? Before or after I have Neil's baby? Or is tonight the last night? Or was last night the last night, but I got in trouble and called you? When does this end, Bryan? Because it will end, right?"

He doesn't look at me. Instead, he gets up, goes to the makeshift minibar he brought along and pours a drink. He downs it and looks back at me. "This will end when I'm through with you."

He's cold and the way he grips that glass makes me think he's angry. After a moment, he turns, and grabs something from his pants pocket before heading to the bathroom. When the door shuts, I spring from the bed and race across the room to see what it was. I pick up his pants and reach into the pocket. My fingertips brush against loose pills, some long, some small. I pull them out and look down at my palm, ready to cry. He's high.

CHAPTER 15

"Do you always go through people's clothes when they're in the bathroom or am I special?" Bryan sounds upset, but he's still got that cocky grin on his face. I take the pills and throw them at him.

"High much?" I grab my clothes and start tugging them on.

"Oh, no you don't." Bryan rushes up to me and we struggle for a moment before he rips my shirt out of my hands and throws it across the room. "We had a deal."

"Fuck you! Fuck your family! Fuck our deal! I hate you! I wish you never showed up again! I can't stand this anymore! I can't!" I'm screaming in his face and manage to get my bra hooked. "Keep the shirt, but I'm not staying and you can't make me. Tell whomever you want. I'm done."

He smiles sadly at the floor and then back at the shirt in his hand. "After everything we've been through, all I get is this shirt?"

"I'm not kidding Bryan." I'm at the door.

"Neither was I. I'd do anything for you." He whispers the last words. "But I can't. Life's not fair, Hallie. I'm doing the best I can and that's all I can tell you. There's a reason I'm not in rehab and why I can walk around with all that shit in my pocket. There's a reason why, and I swore to God I wouldn't tell you. So you can walk away and be offended that I'm a junkie, that I need drugs, but you have to know that I'd throw them all away to keep you here one more day."

I don't understand what he's saying. Bryan's gaze narrows as it meets mine. I call him on it because I think he's bluffing. "Then do it. Buy me for a day and throw all that shit out."

"Done." He empties his pockets, picks up the pills scattered on the carpet, and tosses every single one out into the parking lot. When he slams the door he turns back to me. "I did my part, now you do yours. Strip."

Why does it feel like I've just done something horrible? I do as he says until I'm wearing nothing. He watches me with those greedy green eyes, like he could never get enough. As he steps toward me, he smirks, "It's secret time."

"I have no secrets."

"We both know that's a lie." He laces his arms around my bare waist and presses his hard length against me. I want things I shouldn't want, but I try to stay calm and collected. Inside, I'm thrilled that he tossed his pills for me. He's a druggie and this will help. It will. I know it will.

My gaze darts away and I smile. "There are things you shouldn't know."

"Campone?"

I glance up at him. "Maybe."

We start dancing to music that is only in our minds. It's something from high school, from forever ago, and I swear I can still hear it. Bryan presses his cheek to mine. "Do I need to be watching for him?"

"No one needs to be watching for him."

Bryan swallows hard and pauses. He knows what I mean, there's not a doubt in my mind that he doesn't. A moment later he asks, "Do you regret it?"

"No," my voice doesn't come out because it catches in my throat.

"It sounds like you might."

I lose it. All the emotions I've been repressing bubble up. The words escape before I can stop them. "Bryan, I regret my whole life."

"Don't say that." He presses my face to his and holds me. Our feet stop moving and he kisses the side of my cheek once, then twice. "You're the best thing that ever happened to me."

"Don't." I pull away from him and step away. I'm staring at the worn carpet and the unidentified stains on the flattened pile. "I can't. I just can't." As I move to walk away, he grabs my wrist.

A sincere smile crosses his lips. "You have no idea how much you mean to me, do you?"

"I didn't mean all that much in the past."

He laughs, but I don't look back at him. I sit on the corner of the bed and stare at the ugly painting on the wall. It should have been a happy scene but time and sunlight faded a once bright spot. The paper is yellowed and the frame is chipped. The screws holding it to the wall don't help either. "You've always been so good at lying, Hallie. Especially when it comes to lying to yourself."

"You don't know what you're talking about."

"Bullshit! Hallie, look at me!" Bryan is standing by my shoulder and I hear him let out a rush of air. I assume that he's annoyed with me until I see his reflection in the glass on the frame. His face is contorted and he's clutching his head so hard that I can see every muscle in his body.

I whirl around and jump to my feet. My hands hover above him as if I shouldn't touch him. "What's wrong? Bryan?" I'm nearly crying as I watch him tremble and try to breathe, but his ribs barely move. He reaches out for the bed and sits down hard, clutching his head between his hands.

He stays like that, trying so hard to just breathe, that it kills me. I pull on his shirt and race out into the parking lot barefoot when I'm sure he's not going to die and look for the pills, but the pavement is wet and they've melted. Tears stream from my eyes. I had no idea. Something's wrong with him and I didn't know. I thought he was partying, and acting like a fucking junkie so I made him toss his medicine.

And he did.

For me.

His voice is weak, behind me, as I try to pick up a pill that's melting into nothing. "Leave it."

"I didn't know!" I'm crying. The pill turns to paste in my fingers. Before I can go for another one, he grabs my shoulders and turns me toward him.

"I knew." His voice is trembling and tight. He can barely breathe. "I need to sit down. Come inside."

Bryan throws his arm over my shoulder and we walk back to the bed. He laughs and then grimaces quickly. "I shouldn't have ridden you like that, but it was worth it. You've always been worth it, Hallie."

CHAPTER 16

Bryan is writhing on the bed and in so much pain that tears stream down his cheeks. He won't let me take him to the hospital. He keeps saying they can't do anything, but I can't watch him like this. "Who else knows?"

"No one." He manages the words in short breathes between clenched teeth as his back rises off the mattress again. His hands are balled into fists at his sides as another groan escapes him.

"I need to get your medicine, tell me where to get them." I'm frantic. He's gotten so much worse, so fast. The movement, the time he was with me must have made it worse, because he's so close to screaming out in pure agony that I can't stand it.

"Jon." That's all he says.

Fuck. I hate Jon. Why couldn't he say Trystan? I nod and grab his phone, scroll through his contacts and find Jon Ferro. I dial and wait forever for him to pick up. "Hey shithead, are you still chasing that thing you nailed in high school?"

"I am that thing he nailed in high school. Listen, Bryan is in a lot of pain. His medicine is gone and he needs some now— like right now."

For a second I think he's hung up, but then he asks, "Where are you?" I tell him. "Fuck. I thought you were in jail. Shit, Hallie, shit! Get him wasted until I get there, and do NOT take him to the hospital." That's all Jon says before he hangs up.

I put the phone back on the nightstand and cross the room. Most of the booze Bryan brought is gone, but there's some vodka left. I pour it into a plastic cup and bring it to him. "Here, drink this. It'll help a little bit."

Bryan takes the cup and downs the whole thing. His stomach is empty and that was at least three shots. I take the cup away and set it down on the dresser before sitting next to him. Within seconds, I see his muscles begin to relax. His eyes have been pinched shut for so long that when they flutter open, I nearly cry. "You stayed."

"I'm an arrogant, presumptive asshole. I should never have made you throw those away. I'm so sorry." I bend at the waist, wanting to lie on his chest, but it'll hurt him, so I settle for a kiss over his heart.

He touches the back of my head, smoothing my hair, soothing me. "You didn't know."

"Why didn't you tell me?"

"It's easier to let people assume other things." He watches me and knows how close that statement hits to home. It is easier. It saved me in many ways. Yes, I understand, all too well. I wish I didn't. Bryan's body continues to relax for the next few minutes until Jon arrives.

Jon growls at me as he shoves his way in the room and to Bryan. "You fucking loser. You did her with no meds? You're insane, you know that?" Jon shoves a bunch of pills at his cousin and a glass of water.

Bryan downs them and laughs. As soon as he does it, his hands fly to his ribs like they're sore. "She's worth it."

"You're an asshole."

"I love you too, man."

Jon snorts at that, before turning to me. "How much did you give him to drink?"

"That," I point at the cup. "It was about half full, so what, three shots?"

Jon tries not to smile. "You aren't much of a drinker, are you? That's more like five. No wonder he's not screaming."

As we talk Bryan's eyes close and his body relaxes. I can't help it. I ask Jon, "What's wrong with him?"

"It's not my place to say." Jon looks over at his cousin under the sheets. Bryan lies on his back, his chest slowly rising and falling. His fingers finally uncurl and I know he's asleep.

"Yeah, he didn't tell you either."

"Nope. I haven't got a fucking clue." Jon rubs the back of his neck and stares at the bed. After a long time, he says, "We're going to lose him. This is getting worse.

That's all I know, and I wish to God I didn't. The guy acts like he's got nothing to lose because he doesn't."

CHAPTER 17

We're both standing there, me in Bryan's shirt, and Jon in his leather jacket and black slacks. We form a temporary truce as we watch someone we love fading in front of our eyes. I wish he told Jon. Bryan needs to confide in someone, and I know he had no intention of ever telling me. That's why he blackmailed me--so I'd never know. I smile and tell Jon.

"Yeah, he's a little crazy like that. He probably wanted to be with you and thought blackmail was faster. It never even dawned on the guy to pick up a phone." Jon folds his arms across his chest and adds, "The thing with the car wasn't me.

My mother reported it stolen. By the time I found out, they already picked you up."

"I don't care." I'm done talking to him. "Take your shitty car and all your false sincerity and go puke it up in the parking lot. I know you hate me. The feeling is mutual." I sit next to Bryan and run a finger along his brow, pushing back his hair. I wish I could take this away. I wish I knew how to help him.

Jon snaps, "I should beat the shit out of you for hurting him like that."

"You hit women? Nice." I don't look up. I'm so annoyed at him and his mother. She always hated me and I never knew why.

"I hit whores, and that's what you are, Hallie, so stop pretending. The last thing Bryan needs right now is another liar. Fuck him and leave. Don't make him think you care. Even you're not that cruel."

His words slice through me. I stand to scream at Jon to leave, but he's already through the door. I sit down hard on the side of the bed and sob into my hands. I thought I'd already lost everything, but I hadn't. Bryan was still there, still around to be encountered, and the hope that we might be together again was never fully extinguished from my mind.

That's why I said yes.

That's why I let him blackmail me.

I never wanted to breakup with Bryan in the first place, and now it's too late.

THE PROPOSITION VOL 4

To ensure you don't miss the next installment, text AWESOMEBOOKS to 22828 and you will get an email reminder on release day.

*****

THE FERRO FAMILY MOVIE
Vote now to make it happen!
http://www.ipetitions.com/petition/ferro/

*****

What do you think will happen next?
Go to Facebook and join the discussion!
*****

COMING SOON:

NEW YORK TIMES BESTSELLING AUTHOR

H.M. WARD

the
wedding
contract

THE FERRO FAMILY

THE WEDDING CONTRACT
Coming April 14, 2014

MORE FERRO FAMILY BOOKS

BRYAN FERRO
~THE PROPOSITION~

*****

SEAN FERRO
~THE ARRANGEMENT~

******

PETER FERRO GRANZ
~DAMAGED~

******

JONATHAN FERRO
~STRIPPED~

MORE ROMANCE BOOKS BY

H.M. WARD

DAMAGED

DAMAGED 2

STRIPPED

SCANDALOUS

SCANDALOUS 2

SECRETS

THE SECRET LIFE OF
TRYSTAN SCOTT

And more.

To see a full book list, please visit:
www.SexyAwesomeBooks.com/books.htm

CAN'T WAIT FOR H.M WARD'S NEXT STEAMY BOOK?

⭐⭐⭐⭐⭐

Let her know by leaving stars and telling
her what you liked about
THE PROPOSITION VOL. 3
in a review!

CPSIA information can be obtained at www.ICGtesting.com
Printed in the USA
LVOW07s1630260315

432155LV00005B/465/P